Andrew Carpenter Wheeler

The Iron Trail

Andrew Carpenter Wheeler

The Iron Trail

ISBN/EAN: 9783743465039

Manufactured in Europe, USA, Canada, Australia, Japa

Cover: Foto ©Andreas Hilbeck / pixelio.de

Manufactured and distributed by brebook publishing software
(www.brebook.com)

Andrew Carpenter Wheeler

The Iron Trail

THE IRON TRAIL.

A SKETCH.

BY A. C. WHEELER,

(The "NYM CRINKLE" of the *N. Y. World.*)

> We've sought them where in warmest nooks
> The freshest feed is growing,
> By sweetest springs, and clearest brooks,
> Through honeysuckle flowing :
> Wherever hillsides sloping south
> Are bright with early grasses,
> Or, tracking green the lowland's drouth,
> The mountain streamlet passes.
>
> —WHITTIER.

NEW YORK.

F. B. PATTERSON, PUBLISHER.

1876.

WHY.

I, too, with my soul and body,
We, a curious trio, picking, wandering on our way
Through these shores, amid the shadows, with
The apparitions pressing.
Pioneers, O Pioneers!

—WALT WHITMAN.

"ARE we Americans, or are we not? That's what I'd like to know," cried June.

June's my sister.

She had jumped upon her big Saratoga trunk, and had unconsciously assumed the attitude of the little corporal when he stormed the bridge of Lodi.

"We are!" I cried.

"Then," said June, "where are we going? That's the next thing I'd like to know. Where are we going TO?"

Now she had unconsciously assumed the attitude of the stump speaker in the minstrel band.

"Why, of course we'll go to Europe," I said. "Breathes there an American with soul so dead as to stay in his own country when there's a Centennial?"

"I should hope not," cried Ben, who had just come in.

Ben's my large brother. He stands six feet two; weight, 210 pounds; eyes blue; hair shaved short; manners bluff; style generally A I.

"The thing for us to do is the steam yacht business. Lay in a cargo of canned fruits, take a grand piano, confectionery, fire-works, French cook, brass band, touch at Newport on the way out, Banks of Newfoundland, icebergs, saluted by English steamers, run into Cowes on the other side, go up to Lord Dunderhead's castle, return ball on board next night, Empress of India and the President of the United States drunk standing, then up the Mediterranean, sweep in the whole of the historic sea from Gibraltar to Greece, salute the flags of all nations, flirt with the women of all climes, write our names on everything that's exposed, load up with cashmere shawls, old masters, mummies, cheap statuary, come back when the Centennial is all over, celebrated, satisfied, triumphant! Eh! What?"

"Stop a moment," said June, "I want to hug you."

"Don't hug me," replied Ben; "go and hug the Governor; that's where the pressure must be applied; it'll take from ten to fifteen thousand dollars."

"Is that all?" said the dear girl. "Why, it's dirt cheap. It costs more than that to go to Paris, don't it?"

"Yes, if there's women in the party."

"At all events," continued June, sitting down on her trunk and assuming a meditative look, "we must go somewhere. This is the first time in five years that we haven't had our route made up before the first of April. Do you know that this delay is awful? If any thing should happen to keep us in New York all summer, I should never cease to upbraid myself for my crime and folly to my latest breath."

"My dear June," I remarked, "that's an absurd supposition; whatever happens, that need not take place."

" Why not ?"

" Because we can always hang ourselves or go to Long Branch, and thus at one sublime *coup* avoid New York and the annoyance of waiting for our latest breath."

The mention of Long Branch brought on a general laugh. It always does. I suppose it is because none of us ever go there, and can afford to laugh.

We had a little council of war. Ben was self-confident, cynical, and extravagant. June was suspicious, anxious, and oratorical. I was patient, wise and sweet-tempered, as I always am.

" My American character urges me to action," said June, " and my woman's instinct tells me there is need of it at once."

" What does your woman's instinct see in the way ?" asked Ben.

" Men," replied June. " Oh, if Governors and brothers were only women, there would be no trouble, no delay, no doubts. We'd fly to Paris without a thought or an argument."

" And come back without a red."

" Go and see the head of the family," continued the girl. " If we can't have a yacht, we must at least have three state-rooms ; and we must have them at once. Remember the adage, Procrastination is the—what do ye call it of something."

BUFFALO TRAILS IN WESTERN KANSAS.

" Oh, that's all right," said Ben, in his princely way. " I'll go in, see the Governor and arrange for the state-rooms. Let me see, it's now the eighth of April (looking at his watch as if it were a calendar). We'll start about the first of May. I'd like to be in the Tyrol in June. Wouldn't you ?"

" Anywhere, anywhere, as Hood says, out of the etcetera," replied the pride of the family, pushing him out.

" The truth is," she said to me when Ben was gone, " I must have something to do. I'm stagnating."

Health, fashion, comfort, patriotism, honor, duty, all say we must go abroad.

So it was all fixed. We had put our heads together. Now we would join hands.

Was there ever a Governor that did not fall before such a combination ?

" Never," I cried, as I took a nosegay out of June's hair and put it in my button-hole, preparatory to walking down Broadway.

WHERE.

The great South-western Railroad
  For Colorado, hail!
Bring on your locomotive
  And lay down your iron rail.
Across the rolling prairies
  By steam we're bound to go.
The railroad cars are coming—humming
  Through New Mexico.

THE Governor had it in his leg. Ordinarily, when it took him in the shoulder, we could get along with him; when it settled in his side, we grinned and bore it, for we knew that it would pass over with the first bright, dry day. But when he had it in his leg, it generally staid there until the housekeeper gave notice, and life no longer offered any charms to the cook or the chambermaid, and we had to watch June to prevent her from flinging herself head first into her Saratoga trunk, and letting the lid down with a snap.

When he had it in his leg he was, to put it mildly, transformed from a benevolent and serene patriarch, into a howling and inconsiderate tyrant.

He had it in his leg now, and we had not yet discovered it.

We gathered at the breakfast table, smiling and happy. June looked at Ben. Ben nodded and intimated that the thing was safe in his hands. Then he opened the matter boldly.

"See here," said he, suddenly, "if we're going abroad this summer, we'd better be getting ready; the passages ought to be taken and arrangements made!"

The Governor looked over the top of his paper. He was a little blue under the eyes, and purple about the end of his nose, and white about the lips.

"Who says we're going abroad?" he shouted fiercely. "Show me the man!"

Ben opened his blue eyes wide. June gave a little gasp, as if she already saw herself consigned to Long Branch and infamy.

"If you've got such a notion as that in your heads," he added, looking at all of us with devouring rage, "you're all abroad now!"

Then the housekeeper fled trembling out of the room. A horrid silence fell upon the group, which was not broken by the husky whisper of June in Ben's ear.

"Merciful heavens! he's got it in his leg."

To which Ben, in a desperate sort of way, replied, "I'm afraid he has, and I've got it square between the eyes. I wish you'd have me carried out!"

Presently the Governor, seeing us at his mercy, and actuated by the malign spirit of his leg, returned to the subject.

THE GOVERNOR MAKES AN INHUMAN AND INCENDIARY SPEECH.

"You're a nice lot of Americans, aren't you? Never live in your own country long enough to know anything about it. I'm ashamed of you. Fine exhibition for the centennial year.

You'd like to drag me to Italy again and have me down with the Roman fever, wouldn't you? When I've got a thousand acres of paradise myself, where the wicked cease from troubling and the gouty are at rest. If you've got money enough among you, why go to Italy—go to thunder. But I tell you I'm going to stay inside the Republic this year. There, that'll do on that subject. I don't want to hear a word more."

"But," said June, horror struck, "you don't think seriously of staying in—in New York?"

"Don't I!" he shouted. "If I didn't think seriously, who the deuce would in this family? No, I'm not going to stay here. I'm going—"

We all held our breaths.

"I'M GOING TO COLORADO!"

THE MOST PROMINENT BUILDING IN A KANSAS TOWN.

WHEN.

And in thy right hand lead with thee,
The mountain nymph, sweet Liberty.
And, if I give thee honor due,
Mirth, admit me of thy crew.

—MILTON.

AT first we were stunned. Then we settled into a despairing anger. Then we began to re-cover our senses.

"Going to Colorado!" said June. "Why, he'll have to travel on a dromedary. It's part of the Great American desert. It was that Doctor Lavender who put this notion into his head."

"Oh, he'll get over it in a few days," remarked Ben, with a great effort at carelessness.

But he didn't. He hung to Colorado with the tenacity of a catamount and much of its ferocity.

The result was something that no human being could have foreseen.

In the first place, June, who had tried in vain to win the Doctor over and failed, suddenly veered clear round and came out enthusiastically for Colorado herself.

In the second place, she won both Ben and myself over to her views. And we all went to Colorado.

To tell how this astonishing girl accomplished all this would compel me to write an essay on the illimitable female resources.

Her first step was in the direction of the Governor. She got some kind of an emotional lever under him. But for the first time it failed to move him.

"It's no use," he said, "I've got to carry my leg somewhere into a climate that will subdue it. An ocean voyage is worse than the rack. I want the sky of Italy, the air of Switzerland, the scenery of Norway, the water of Ems, the society of Nature—I can't get them anywhere but in Colorado, and there I'm going."

Seeing that he was immovable, she, like a true woman, ceased her assault and established an alliance.

"Somebody's got to go with him," she said, to Ben and me. "It will never do to let him go alone, for if he escapes the Indians, grizzly bears and border ruffians, he will be sure to fall into the pitiless clutch of some wild Western widow—and then what would life be worth to us, I'd like to know? Somebody has got to be sacrificed—as usual it is a woman. I'll go with him."
[Tears.]

When woman sets an example of heroism in her vital, impulsive way, man takes off his coat lumberingly and imitates her.

"By Heavens!" said Ben, "you shall not expose yourself to the horrors of Colorado unpro-tected, so long as you have a brother. If you must do this insane thing, I shall not let you go alone. A man can die but once."

8

"No! No!" cried June, "your life is worth too much to the world. It cannot spare you. Let me perish alone. I shall never be missed."

"Not if I know myself," said Ben. "If there is any wild Western perishing to be done, I must be counted in. I shall commence practicing with the bow and arrows at once, and saturating myself with quinine."

"It will never do to break up the family in that way," I began. "Whatever we do, let us all stick together—especially in a misfortune of this kind. I shall go too."

Having accomplished this much, what does June do next but throw herself into the Colorado business, heart and soul.

For instant and complete adaptation to any emergency, I would back that girl against the world.

She laid in a stock of maps, gazetteers, guide-books, railroad pamphlets and Western newspapers. She crammed, she inquired, she took the whole tour in charge. She became mistress of the situation.

And neither Ben nor I could understand it.

The utmost we could do was to submit.

However, I noticed that Ben, now that his attention was called to it, took a growing interest in the great American wilderness as he called it. Inquiries about Colorado only served to awaken in him fresh curiosity, and he went about talking in an absurd strain, that was too ironical to be sincere, and too ridiculous to be offensive, about the glorious freedom of the Alkali Plains, the health-giving sports of the bottom lands, and the indescribable delight there was in going beyond the reach of civilization, and the sound of the church-going what d'ye call it, as June phrased it.

So it was finally all settled that we were to start for Colorado on the 12th.

Several days were given up to preparation; to sad farewells; to the winding up of a thousand pretty home machines that were expected to run till we came back; to the making of outfits; to the answering of inquiries, and to the severing of the ties that bound us.

The Governor had his life insured, and made a new will; he also sat for an imperial picture at the request of the Board of Trustees of St. Angelus' Church, and June laid in a stock of albums and other rubbish.

On the twelfth of April, we left New York in a snow storm, a rather gloomy party. "Rushing" June said, "to the what d'ye call 'ems, that we know not of." But, at any rate, leaving New York.

HOW?

Yet I rejoice; a myrtle fairer than
E'er grew in Paphos, from the bitter weeds
Lifts its sweet head into the air, and feeds
A silent space with ever-sprouting green.
—KEATS.

ON the fourteenth, we were in St. Louis for the first time in our lives.

All the way out, the Governor had been the wonder and delight of the passengers who reveled in strong exhibitions of character. His leg performed the most amazing feats; it overturned a Pullman car conductor—a thing that was never done before; it got a train-boy into trouble; it precipitated a political quarrel with an old gentleman in the next section, and brought tears to the eyes of June more than once.

The only breeze of comfort the poor girl got, was from a gentleman by the name of Bellamy —introduced to our party at the start—who assured her that the leg would be born again if it ever reached Colorado.

Bellamy was a young Englishman—a liberal, full of his country's pluck and fiber, and a fortunate acquisition to our party. As he had been all over the world, and liked that portion of it best which was lying at the base of the Rocky Mountains, and was cultivated, handsome and entertaining, he soon became an accepted member of our group.

One incident occurred in St. Louis that is worth mentioning. We met the Dollipers there— old New York acquaintances. *The* Dolliper used to be considered a dashing widow. She had gone into the hemp business with her only son, and had quite a large plantation just outside the city. We found the town quite gay, and as June had good company, there did not appear to be any immediate prospect of leaving it. Ben and I were getting tired of it at the end of three days, and proposed to the Governor to set out again. To our amazement he said he had concluded on the whole to remain in St. Louis. He was interested in some experiments in the culture of hemp; we could go on without him. When June heard this, she opened her blue eyes wide.

"It's the Dolliper," said she. "Haven't you noticed the Governor's been putting pomatum on his hair? Look at him, there he comes! He got a new hat! That's a designing woman. We must start at once."

Exactly how she managed it, neither Ben nor I never knew, but manage it she did, and we set out for Kansas City the next day. I thought the Governor looked a little sheepish as if he'd been outwitted or reprimanded, but I may have been mistaken.

Our travels, however, began at Kansas City. From that point, our journey was an entirely new one, and eventful enough to form the topic of my book.

Once in this beautiful city,—lying in the exact geographical center of the Republic,—a double ray of sunshine broke upon us. First of all, the Governor was seen to smile. Then we met with genuine spring weather that had a smell of blossoms in it. Something in the air stirred us. June broke out into song, and Ben wanted to buy a house.

Bellamy took him out upon the bluffs and pointed out the promised land, lying in green levels as far as color and beauty were discernible.

"It looks like wilderness at last," said Ben. "But I'm not sure of it. Something tells me we shall find opera-houses and railroad depots where we expect to meet savages and

silence. I despair of ever getting beyond the reach of paper collars and condensed milk. The great American wilderness is a humbug.

REMARKS OF BELLAMY ON METEOROLOGY.

"The State of Kansas is, in my opinion, the most remarkable evidence of the speed and splendor of your civilization, anywhere to be found in the States. Kansas is only eleven years old as a State, and twenty years ago, you were cutting each other's throats here in the most approved barbarism.

WHAT THEY DO NOT BELIEVE EAST.

"I believe the marvelous growth of the territory into a garden of civilization is owing, in a great measure, to the air. It stimulates the inhabitants just as it does vegetation. If it had been settled by Frenchmen it would have intoxicated them. We should have had a new republic in every county, barricades and opera bouffé all along the border, and the beauty and chivalry of the great West quoting Victor Hugo, guzzling absinthe, and jumping into all the rivers from mere excess of animal spirits. But these Americans—do you know how they utilize all this fine air? I'll tell you. When they feel exhilarated, they rush out and turn over another section of wild land. If the spirit of the air moves them strongly, they put up another school-house, or stick in another tree. If the excitement runs high, they build another hundred miles of railroad or open a new coal-mine.

"When you get out into this State, you'll see the water-mills all over, by which every zephyr is made to add to the productiveness of the country. It's very much the same with the people. Every ounce of oxygen means a gallon pumped or a pound raised."

THE AUTHOR TAKES UP THE THREAD.

After these remarks, Ben said he felt like corroborating them by raising a few ounces himself. Ben is of a jocular turn.

Bellamy, on the contrary, was a matter-of-fact fellow, whose veins were full of statistics, and whose heart beat as correctly as a metronome.

Coming back from the bluffs to the hotel, we met the Governor, surrounded by a crowd of evil-disposed persons, evidently intent upon lynching him. Ben felt for his revolver. But Bellamy advised him to hold on. As we came up, one of them slipped a card into my hand.

BEWARE OF THE U. P.

"They take us for Massachusetts men," I cried, "and this is a warning not to start a U. P. (Union Press) in Kansas. They're border ruffians."

Another of the fellows got hold of Ben. "Look here," he said, "didn't you come by the O. R. & P. M. P. straight?"

"No, sir," replied Ben, "I didn't come by it straight or crooked, I haven't got such a thing about me, haven't seen it, don't know what it is."

"Oh! go 'way and let the gent be," cried another; "don't you see he's a K. P."

"Gentlemen," observed the Governor, with dignity, "one word: I assure you, on my honor, we are not K. P.'s, and have no affiliation with U. P.'s. You mistake us entirely, we have never meddled with Ku Klux organizations or local prejudices, we are simply traveling for pleasure.

"Pleasure!" they all shouted in chorus. "Ah ha! then there's only one thing to do!" And with that they all poked their circulars into our faces.

"Never go back on the O. R. & P. M. P.!" yelled one.

"You'll go back on yourselves if you don't patronize the F. E. & W. R. St. L. K. C. & N. R. R.!" screamed another.

This last eruption of Western eloquence overcame us, and we fled in all directions.

The Governor took refuge in a drug store, where he was pursued by a K. P., who committed an assault and a half-sheet poster on him.

Ben got safely to the hotel and locked his door just as an O. R. & P. M. P. was shoved under it.

I was caught on a corner, and four of them held me, while a fifth read to me the horrors of the U. P.

With my blood curdling, I broke into Ben's room afterward, where the rest of our party had assembled, and exclaimed, "In heaven's name, what does this mean—is it all over?"

"Over," said Ben, summoning all his Eastern wit, "why, its only the initial trouble."

A GOOD SIGN ON THE PLAINS.

"Yes, but the horrible O. R. & P. M. P. It may at any moment rise up in our path."

"Not unless there's a freshet," said Bellamy; "it only means the 'The Old Reliable and Popular Missouri Pacific Railroad.'"

June broke out in a loud laugh, and the Governor joined her.

The sight of his merriment put us all in excellent spirits.

"But we must go by one of these railroads, I suppose," said he; "we'd better decide at once."

REMARKS BY THE REST OF THE COMPANY.

Ben. The way to go to Colorado is to take the California route, Union Pacific, come down to Denver, and there you are.

June. That's one way. Another is to go down the Mississippi, and come up through Mexico on pack-mules. In that case, the more haste the less—what d'ye call it?

Governor. Boys, give me that map of the United States. See here, that's Colorado, isn't it?

"Yes," we all said, bending over the map.

"Well, that green square is Kansas, isn't it? I can't see very well without my glasses."

"Yes," we all said.

"Then," said the Governor, taking Ben's pencil, "I'll show you my route. I'm for the P. & D. W. That is—the pleasantest and directest way."

With that he drew a pretty straight line from Kansas City, on the Missouri, to Pueblo, in Colorado.

Ben. Do you propose to build a road for our party?

Bellamy. By George, he won't have to. There's one already. It's under his pencil mark. General pantomime of examination.

Grand Chorus. It's the Atchison, Topeka, and Santa Fé!

So it was.

Governor. You forget that I want to see my land, and the only way to see it is to go where it is. Besides, Southern Kansas is in about the same latitude as Richmond, Virginia. Why should I take my leg into the inhospitable North? Why, you innocent youngsters, did you ever hear of an intelligent party coming all the way out here, without finding out first which way they were going? Do you suppose I hadn't made up my mind before I left New York, and bought our tickets over the Atchison, Topeka, and Santa Fé road? I'm an M. T. D. B. T. W.—that is, a man that don't do business that way. Didn't you know there was an Eastern agency on the corner of Broadway and Park Place, where you can find out all about this road and its Kansas lands?"

June. Yes, but pa, what are we going to do while you are examining your land? We don't want to examine land, you know.

Ben. No, that would be rather absurd.

Governor. You don't want to do anything but gad. See here, you blessed runagates, I'm going to offer a prize to the one who makes the best use of the time. I'm going to set an example to American fathers who live in the centennial year. I'll give the two thousand acres to the man or woman in my family who gets up the most information, and comes out of the West knowing the most about it.

"How's that for an offer, Mr. Bellamy?"

Mr. Bellamy. A very liberal offer, sir, in my opinion.

Ben. By George! What's the land worth?

Governor (with a sly twinkle). Why, that comes under the head of Western information.

June (firing up). Bought at $1.25 an acre, and offered at $5.00.

Governor. Well, you can't have it for $10.00.

Ben. But you'll make it a present to one of us?

Governor. If one of you earns it. I will, by Jove!

When the Governor used this rare mythologic oath, we knew—as June would say—that his word was as good as his what d'ye call it.

June. But we needn't hurry away from Kansas City, need we? I'm decidedly in favor of moving by easy stages if I am to gather information.

This conversation put a new face on affairs. June ransacked the town for agricultural reports, and that night we found her at the hotel, footing up figures and refusing to go to the opera-house and see *Colonel Sellers.*

Before she retired, however, a letter was shown her from the Governor. It read thus:

"Hear you are stopping over in Kansas City. I'm glad of it, because I shall overtake you. Count me in your party.   OLIVE DOLLIFER."

"Now," remarked June, "as I said before, we ought to hurry away from here. If we want to see the West—why waste time in a city?"

THE FIRST FARM-SITE SPECULATORS—PRAIRIE DOGS.

A BLOSSOMING WILDERNESS.

Her dark dilating eyes expressed
The broad horizons of the West;
Her speech dropped prairie flowers: the gold
Of Harvest wheat about her rolled.

—WHITTIER.

THE Atchison, Topeka & Santa Fé Railroad, which is comparatively a new road, has two branches leaving the Missouri River at Kansas City and at Atchison. These branches meet at Topeka, the capital of the State, distant sixty-six miles from the former, and fifty miles from the latter city.

I was making a memorandum of this in my book as we were leaving Kansas City. June looked over my shoulder.

"What was it they called the trick of getting your lesson by proxy, when you went to school?"

"Smouching," I replied.

"Well, that isn't a pleasant word. Tell me about the railroad."

"Well, that's a nice proposition," I exclaimed. "Such amazing impudence is—"

"Is allowable only in a sister."

"Well," I said, "take your pencil. The road, I mean this road, is chiefly remarkable for its route, its terminus and its condition. It runs through the garden of the world, presented to it by the United States of America, in the shape of a land grant, which, for value, has never been exceeded by any similar government endowment. It comprises, in fact, two million, five hundred acres of land lying in alternate sections, twenty miles each side of the route. If you want to know what kind of land it is look out the window."

JUNE'S LITTLE RHAPSODY ON KANSAS.

"There's something peculiar in the beauty of a cultivated prairie that baffles description. The level lines and low down horizon have a charm that is unexpected. In the first place, the colors are brighter and deeper than in any other picture. The earth shows long rich patches of blue-black earth, against which the emerald green of the young wheat-fields gleams with a rare brilliancy, and over which the blue sky—a deep unruffled ultramarine—arches itself in unobstructed splendor. Then the broad unbroken sunshine. No massed shadows; every thing in a bath of brightness. The sense of space, the freedom of vision and the constant impression that one is in an illimitable mead, and that motion is unaccompanied by exertion,—an illusion due in great measure to the stimulating air,—all serve to make the charm an entirely new one, and one that appeals to all the impulses no less than the senses."

"That will never do," I said, when she had read it to me.

"Isn't it true?"

"O yes, but the Governor doesn't want the true and beautiful. He desires the actual and literal. Leave out about the emerald green, and say, rolling prairie of black loam from three to six feet deep, resting on limestone. So rich, in fact, that plenty of men have paid for their land by their first wheat-crop."

"Isn't it just like Illinois?"

"No; Illinois is troubled with wet bottom lands in its southern part, and the cold winds from Lake Michigan in the northern counties shorten the season materially. The valleys through which the A. T. & S. F. R. R. runs are singularly free from great deposits of alluvium, and consequently from miasm and fever and ague."

June folded up her paper.

"Wait; I'll get it," she said.

"What?"

"Information!"

When we got to Topeka she insisted on a horse. That having been bought, she resolved to live in the saddle, and seriously proposed to the Governor to make the rest of the journey on horse-back. Not suc-

WATER-TANK ON THE A. T. & S. F. R. R.

ceeding in this scheme, she inveigled Ben, and together they scoured the prairies for miles around, coming back to the hotel flushed and hungry, and bursting with oxygen and information.

Topeka is a model prairie city, of ten thousand people, watered by the Arkansas, that brawls through it, and fringed with orchards and farms, just at this time, blossomy and bright. It is provided with several first-class hotels, is lit with gas, and its streets are laid out in broad level avenues. Nothing more inviting than this bright garden city, with its residences already embowered in fruit-trees and flowers, can be found in the State.

It is, however, but the first of a series of sixty towns along the A. T. & S. F. R. R., all of which have been projected with the same liberality and taste, and all of which are progressing toward metropolitan significance with marvelous rapidity.

SOMETHING LIKE AN ADVENTURE.

The improvement in the Governor's health was magical. He assumed robust airs, and began to talk like a pioneer. He proposed to me to ride over the country with him and see if we could discover his land. Somehow he had an idea that for a New York man to see his Western land, would be an immense practical joke. So the next morning, a spanking team was provided, and we set out, after getting our bearings at the land office.

It was a fifteen miles' drive across an undulating country, every inch of which, with the exception of the roadways and water-courses, was alive with the growing wheat-crop, now eight and ten inches high. A soft, south wind swept over the country. It was vitalizing and balmy, and filled us with new life.

It is a most delicious sensation to find one's own Governor a companionable fellow, who asks you for a light, who cracks a joke, and hums a tune, and tells a story, and calls you "my boy."

"This, my boy," he said, pointing to the peach orchards and luxuriant hedges, "is the grasshopper country. They told us in the East that it was devastated, cleaned out, eaten up, root and branch!"

We stopped a moment to watch a man turning the sod in a new quarter section. He sat upon his comfortable plough driving a magnificent team of horses, and the black earth rolled over beneath him in a long, rich wave. He wore a pair of butternut trousers and a hickory shirt. Half a mile farther on stood the farm-house, a simple frame cottage, flanked by the well and stable. In the garden-plot laid out adjacent, a woman was hoeing. She wore an old-fashioned sun-bonnet and a loose calico gown. Her round, brown arms were bare, and the breeze wrapped her drapery round her as if in pure admiration of her lusty outlines.

After riding all the morning through a delightful pastoral country, the Governor arrived at what he pleased to call his share of Eden. It is true, it looked very much like all the rest of Paradise about us, except that Adam had not yet put his plough into it. Wild grass waved as far as the eye could reach, and along the stream that ran through it, there was a fringe of cottonwood, burr oak, and walnut timber. On all sides it was bounded by cultivated farms.

Just as we turned our horses' heads toward a farm-house that gleamed through the distant trees, there appeared upon the crest of the rolling land about half a mile to the east of us, two figures on horseback.

"Indians, as I'm a sinner," said the Governor.

He was right. I saw at a glance by the way they rode their ponies, by the fluttering feathers, and above all, by the long decorated lances that they held in their hands, that they were Cheyenne or Sioux braves, and that we were lost. Without further parley, we

RAWHIDE-FRONTED DUG-OUT—WESTERN KANSAS.

set out at break-neck speed for the farm-house. The south wind rose to a blast as we breasted it in our mad flight. The astonished prairie-chickens and plovers rose in clouds from under our horses' feet. As I was driving, I could only wait for the Governor to make the reconnoissance.

"They're gaining on us," he said. "Have you got your pistol with you?"

"No," I replied, "I left it on my table for a paper-weight."

We could hear their horses' hoofs now, and in spite of the wind, their blood-thirsty yells reached us at intervals.

"By jove," cried the Governor, "one of 'em's a squaw. It's no use killing the horses, we'll have to defend ourselves as best we can."

Then a round, English voice came to us.

"To, ho! Ille ho! We don't want your blood, it's in our veins already!" This, with a little scream of feminine laughter at the end of it.

We pulled up. The Governor and I looked each other in the eyes.

"I thought," said he, "that would be the only way to test their horsemanship."

"Yes," said I, "I understood the joke."

"What in the name of wonder did you run away for?" cried June, as she came up, waving an eighteen foot corn stalk, upon which the dried leaves fluttered like pennons.

For a moment there was no answer; we stood up in the vehicle and looked at the Amazon in silent amazement.

Then Ben slid off his horse, tossed the bridle to June, and plunging into the grass, was lost to sight for three minutes. Nothing but his legs and arms being momentarily visible. We could hear him, however, rolling and snorting as if with excess of prairie oxygen. Then he came out feeling better.

At last the Governor managed to say:

"Running away! nonsense! Did you think we were running away from you?"

But it was impossible to get anything out of the madcaps but laughter, until we all turned back, and at their suggestion, made our way leisurely to what June was pleased to call the ranche of a hardy son of what d'ye call it, that lay on the north of our estate.

JUNE MARSHALS HER FACTS.

The hardy son of toil proved to be a friend of Bellamy's by the name of Markham, and they both rode out to meet us. In Mr. Markham's little house, a dinner was spread, and over that hospitable board, a fine little dispute arose.

The Governor, flushed with Kansas air, a little piqued at his adventure, and probably infected with the utilitarian spirit of the country, precipitated it.

"I came out here," said he, "not to scurry around and practice the war whoop, but to get facts."

"How many did you get?" asked June.

"How many! why the air's full of them. A man breathes information here if he's got sound lungs."

"So does a woman. I was bound that it should not be said, when I went back, that I had not seen the land," exulted June. "There was a man in butternut clothes that we saw ploughing in a field—about six miles south—"

"Yes," said the Governor, "we stopped and studied him."

"And we interviewed him," rejoined June. "He came from Southern Illinois broken down with low fever, and his wife an invalid through rheumatism. He paid $7.75 an acre for that land, with eleven years time to do it. He got in fifty acres of winter wheat the first year and sold it at $1.15 a bushel. He cut one thousand, two hundred and fifty bushels, and pocketed

$500.00 clear of all expenses. The next year, he got in two hundred acres, and commenced building his house. The third year, he paid for his land, and lent some of his money at 7 per cent. I told him I had a prospective interest in these two sections, and he offered me $10.00 an acre for them."

We all looked at her. She never was half so handsome as now. Her eyes sparkled, her cheeks glowed, her words pulsed with a new enthusiasm.

Mr. Markham stared at her with amazement. The Governor was astonished. Bellamy smiled to himself.

" Facts !" she continued. " Why, this State of Kansas is two hundred miles wide, and four hundred miles long. It is bigger than New York and Indiana put together, or than the whole of New England. There are over fifty-two million acres in it, and only a little over four millions have been improved ; simply because the facts don't circulate East, and men when they come here never go back to report them."

" They probably freeze to death in the winter," said the Governor.

They'd be likely to, in a climate where the cattle are left out all winter, and where 5,000 Mennonites keep themselves warm by burning hay, where the weather is coldest.

After that, the Governor gave it up, and the girl had it all her own way.

We spent three days in Topeka, and just before setting out, June told me that she and Ben had ridden all over the Governor's property; made, in fact, a thorough survey of it, and a map.

Whereupon, I began to suspect that none of us had ever quite appreciated June.

The fact is, we never appreciate any of them till they get woke up.

·

ALONG THE ROAD.

Give me a field where the unmowed grass grows;
Give me fresh corn and wheat; give me serene
moving animals, teaching content:
Give me nights perfectly calm as on high
Plateaus west of the Mississippi.
—WALT. WHITMAN.

To properly understand the nature of the ride from Topeka to Pueblo, one must bear in mind that the country between the Missouri River and the base of the Rocky Mountains is a rolling champaign six hundred miles wide, which rises from an elevation of 560 feet above the sea, at Kansas City, to five thousand three hundred feet, at the Mountains. The A. T. & S. F. Railroad ascends this magnificent declivity at the average rate of twelve feet to the mile. For 200 miles the track passes through what is unquestionably the richest, as well as the most beautiful and healthy bottom and meadow land in the world. The Cotton-wood and Arkansas valleys furnish almost unbroken groves of cotton-wood, walnut, oak, pecan, hackberry, box elder, soft maple, mulberry, honey-locust, wild plum, crab, and buck-eye timber.

The twenty-two miles of road-bed in Shawnee County intersect as fine a pastoral picture as the oldest agricultural district can show. The road itself is remarkably well built, of fifty-six pound splice-jointed iron, oak ties (cut in the State); Howe truss bridges (of which there are sixty between Atchison and Granada), stone culverts, and rock ballast, with continuous side-ditching.

Without attempting the description of the sixty towns that have sprung up along the route, and which show the school-house and the church long before the smaller buildings are visible, let me here borrow June's description of the ride to Pueblo.   ·

JUNE AS A DESCRIPTIVE WRITER.

At the distance of two hundred or two hundred and fifty miles west of Kansas City, we approached what may be called the present western limit of arable culture. The morning of the second day's travel reveals a change. The buffalo trails stretch out across the limitless levels in crossing and converging lines. The yellow, air-cured hay of the gramma grass is not yet altogether hidden by the green spears. The dry, white beds of the water-courses, strewn with bowlders, gleam at us with comfortless and voiceless sterility. The buffalo skeletons, bleached and dismembered, multiply close to the track. There has been an occasional cry of "antelope" from the train-boy, and we have strained our eyes, in the direction of pointing fingers, to see a shadowy herd moving indistinctly in the distance, and then mysteriously disappearing. And we have dashed through the prairie dog settlements so often that we no longer smile at their comical antics, or endeavor to knock them off their mounds with our pocket-pistols.

Nor is this second day's change confined to appearances. More than one sense perceives the climatic transition. The air itself, all along wonderfully transparent, is now curiously crystalline and dry. Without the sting of humidity, the breezes in their roughest moods leave only the remembrance of a caress for those invalids who sit upon the car platforms. And if the train stops,—as it will at every one of those water-tanks, that rise like so many miniature forts, and ride at us with increasing size over the horizon,—and we get out upon the hard, dry sod to stretch our limbs, the awful, measureless stillness of desolation settles upon us,—here where the garish hours hang heavy in the luxurious monotony, even the atmosphere is tuneless, save when it borrows a wild moan or two from the telegraph wires. The eye, in vain, endeavors to measure the parallel undulations of the earth as they fade in successive tints into the impalpable blues and grays

SHIP OF THE PLAINS AT SEA.

of the far distance,—still dotted—such is the wonderful achromatic translucency of this atmosphere—with the sage-bush.

It is, at least, three hundred miles across this silent immovable sea, and as we glide over its surface, wearied with its immensity, and yet fascinated with its green waves that run past us,—past us, all day, and seem to flow together far behind, and swallow up the faint, vanishing point of the shining railroad track,—we think, with pity, of those earlier voyagers toiling across this waterless waste in what has been aptly called the Ship of the Plains,—watching, for weary days and weeks, for a glimpse of those cool peaks which, in another hour or two, will lift their spectral outlines, for us, out of the western ether.

That once familiar object on the plains, the canvas-covered emigrant wagon, still crawls occasionally westward, and we see its white top, now and then, far ahead for a while, and presently far behind, diminishing to a gleaming speck, and finally no longer distinguishable from the little piles of bones that dot the distance.

To its weary occupants nothing can be more welcome than the moist oases of the railroad tanks, or that other sign, looming up above the horizon like a burnt tree, but bearing the inscription, "One Mile to R. R. Station. Food and Water."

If we stop at a little station called La Junta, about twenty-one miles west of the old cattle trading-place of Las Animas, we shall strike what is left of the old Santa Fé trail and business, and see the Ship of the Plains in dock, loading for a southern voyage. Here are large storehouses which feed these unwieldy transports with merchandise for New Mexico and Arizona. When loaded, they roll leisurely out across the country, drawn invariably by oxen, and driven by the equally bovine greasers. And the last that is seen of them are the canvas sails as they disappear slowly over the undulating country. It will take them from two weeks to two months to make the voyage, and then they will re-load with wool, hides, and ore, and set out upon their return trip.

La Junta is at present the shipping-point on our line of travel, but it is one of the peculiarities of a new country that these rendezvous move on with the railroad. It is only a year or two ago that Las Animas was the center for the herders, cattle shippers and "greasers." But whatever the point, the character derived from this class remains the same. Greasers and cow-boys are as unlike as it is possible to imagine men, in all but their love of gambling and whisky. I had an opportunity to make a passing sketch of the former at La Junta. He seemed to me to be a creature instinctively aware of the deterioration of his stock, and who had long since made up his mind to dodge as many of the hard knocks of life as possible, and submit servilely to those that he could not avoid. His face is invariably of one type, a tawny, lethargic index of low cunning, dull sensuality and indolence. He preserves the long straight hair and high cheek bones that his mothers borrowed from Indian stock, while his dress and his gait and his character betray the Mexican. Under great stress he does a great deal of simple drudgery, but he does it exactly as do the mules he rides, and when it is over he goes with his fellows and sits in the sun to stare vacantly at the ground or into the air.

As for the land which the Railroad Company offers along this whole distance, the settlements offer the most conclusive evidence of its availability, its fertility and its many resources for all the uses of man. But in order to understand the marked change which takes place after passing the present arable limit and reaching what is at present part of the great plains, and to do away with one of the greatest bugaboos of the East, it must be understood that the apparent sterility of

SHIP OF THE PLAINS IN DOCK.

these plains is not a thing to count upon, nor are the isolated patches of alkali such a dreadful affair as they are represented, and as they doubtless prove to be west of the main range of the Rocky Mountains and even farther north in the State of Kansas.

In the first place, the aridity of the climate west of Fort Dodge, as has been proved by a similar change farther east, will be modified, if not altogether prevented, by tillage and tree-planting.[*]

SHIP OF THE PLAINS AT ANCHOR.

As for the alkali, it only needs the rain-fall to distribute it, and as it contains all the salts and phosphates which elsewhere are dumped upon the land at heavy expense, its presence in limited

GREASER'S WHEELBARROW.

quantities is an evidence of mineral richness. I saw near Fort Dodge, potatoes and corn growing luxuriantly out of what had been an alkali patch, but which a determined man had irrigated by means of a wind-mill pump.

In a word, all that the great plains need to redeem them—if the conversion of the finest grazing lands into farms may be called redemption—is the plough.

At Las Animas, we visited a dug-out, which is a rude habitation made out of a hole in the ground, and when the proprietor is luxurious, is fronted with hides

[*] The State of Kansas has been divided into three rain-fall belts. By reference to the map, the reader can mark them easily. By drawing a line north and south, that will pass through Fort Riley and the city of Topeka, and another following the western boundary of Ellis County, the divisions are apparent. Observations continued for a series of years show that the mean by seasons for the whole State compared with the mean of each belt, give a rain-fall in the middle and western belts one-third less than the eastern. To this it is but proper to add the testimony of J. A. Anderson, President of the State Agricultural College of Kansas. He says: "Those regions, which less than ten years ago, were generally believed to lack sufficient rain for profitable agriculture, are exactly the ones that are now yielding the most remunerative crops. The Great American Desert theory is getting very thin. The boundaries of this geographical bugaboo have so rapidly receded before the plough, that especially with the absolutely dry seasons of California in view, we are not prepared to deny that the western belt, in addition to its superior stock advantages, may yet be found possessed of better grain and fruit qualities than are now conceded."

and decorated with horns. The owner of this establishment, a lank, tawny, sinewy fellow, proved to be an intelligent book-keeper from Detroit, who had suffered with pulmonic disease, and had been given over by his physician. Fortunately, he was a fellow of some will. It was die or rough it. He chose to rough it, and his wife abetted him. They sold out, came here, bought a ranche, excavated a house, regained health, and were happy. This man owned about six hundred cattle. He lived in the saddle, and when we asked him if he did not miss the comforts of society, he said, "Yes, especially the doctors' bills."

Our ride through Kansas chanced to be at the time the farmers along the line of the A. T. & S. F. road were collecting specimens for the Centennial Exhibition, and of their products we were thus

SAILORS RESTING, OR THE GREASERS' LEISURE.

enabled to examine the wheat, corn, oats, castor bean, and countless other products which have since amazed the visitors to the Philadelphia exposition.†

† Since our party has returned, and most of these sheets have gone to the printer, we have visited the Kansas building on the Fair grounds, and fully concur in this statement cut from the Philadelphia correspondence of the N. Y. *World*: "The exhibit made in this building of the products of Kansas from the lands of the A. T. & S. F. road is simply amazing, when we consider how recently that State was a howling wilderness. One has only to pass into this literal bower of Ceres to understand at a glance how magical is the productive power of a railroad managed in the interest of the settler. No other purely agriculture display upon the grounds compares with this from Southern Kansas, either in luxuriant growth, or the variety of products."

PUEBLO.

Once we were stepping a little this way and a little that way: now we are, as it were, in a balloon, and do not think so much of the point we have left, or the point we would make, as of the liberty and glory of the way.
—EMERSON.

FROM Topeka to Pueblo is a steady climb of nearly six hundred miles to the upland plateau of North America. The grade is of the average ascent of ten feet to the mile. When, therefore, the tourist gets to Pueblo, the present terminus of the Atchison, Topeka & Santa Fé road, he is over six thousand feet above the sea-level.*

But he has not arrived at this altitude without undergoing a marked change of spirits. With the increased rarification of the air (due to the elevation), there comes an exhilaration, a buoyancy, an increase of animal spirits, that indicate how effectually the burden of the atmosphere has been lifted from weak shoulders.

There were two or three coughing invalids in the train when we started; they were going to the Colorado Springs by the advice of their doctors. The change in the symptoms, and in the

NEW TIMES ON THE BORDER—SOUTH PUEBLO.

conduct of these sufferers, as we advanced westward, must have been noticed by all the passengers. One of them, a young girl of eighteen, much emaciated, and very weak, insisted upon getting out at one of the water stations, and she roamed about, picking up specimens of wild sage and the early flowers, and we could see her from the car windows, inhaling the dry air with unmistakable pleasure. She had the sympathy of everybody, and everybody, I am sure, noticed with genuine satisfaction how her spirits improved. When we got out at Pueblo, she bade us good-bye with a glad face, and assured us that she was going to get well.

* Pueblo, one of the chief towns, and the natural metropolis of Colorado, had increased from 800 population, in 1870, to 3,500 in 1873. It now has over ten thousand inhabitants. But this is not even comparable to the rate of increase along the Arkansas valley and the eastern section of the A. T. & S. F. road. where they point you out towns of five and six thousand people as "two-year-olds," and "four-year-olds;" thus preserving the nomenclature of the ranchmen even in their sociology.

Pueblo is a quaint town, with the New England village grafted upon the old Spanish settlement. Part of it lies in the valley, and part (this is the future part) upon a beautiful plateau. You miss the green and blossoming freshness of the Kansas towns; its white, dusty streets and low adobe houses do not compare favorably with the spic span cottages of the Cotton-wood and lower Arkansas Valleys.

But one does not need to study long, to know that it will sooner or later be the metropolis of Southern Colorado—the gate-way through which all the enormous travel to the rich mining regions of San Juan and New Mexico must flow; the objective point of all those tourists who visit the parks and canyons of the Rocky Mountains, and the stopping-place of the thousands who are even now selecting this southern route to California. Pueblo, in ten years, will be a large and wealthy city, with the whole of Kansas pouring its produce through its streets into the South-west.

The Denver and Rio Grande (narrow gauge) Railway runs nearly north and south along the eastern slope of Colorado. If we are tourists and invalids, we go north to the Springs, or to Denver. If we are desirous of seeing the mines, we go south, taking the D. & R. G. R. R., and thence by coach or saddle-horse to San Juan.

I am sorry to say that we narrowly avoided a family row at Pueblo. Ben insisted that we should go to the mines, and the Governor insisted, with equal force, that we should go north to

OLD TIMES ON THE BORDER—RICE'S RANCH.

Colorado Springs. A high debate raged; June listened to both sides impartially; Bellamy was on the fence; he had not yet made up his mind whom it was safest to disagree with.

"I've heard too much about these mines," said Ben, "to come out here and turn away from them when they're right under my nose."

"But I didn't come out here to see mines," shouted the Governor. "I couldn't tell one if I did see it. What I want are canyons, passes, gulches, gardens of the gods, peaks, parks, natural springs. Hang it, I came out for a sanitarium; I didn't come for a topographical survey. I don't want to investigate claims. I want to get well."

"All of which you can do by going south as well as north," rejoined Ben. "The marvelous gold fields of Southern Colorado are just now the most interesting subject that the Western country affords."

"Yes, but I won't travel in a coach and sleep in a tent," says the Governor.

"No," adds June, "that's too much to ask."

"Then," says Ben, "I suppose I'll have to go it alone."

It was finally arranged that he should go down into the mining country, while we went north, and that we should afterward meet him half way, at Canyon City.

"You'll be sorry," he said, to June, "that you didn't take my advice."

"No, I will not," persisted that stubborn girl.

Ben left on Thursday. On Friday morning we were just leaving the hotel in Pueblo for the train, when the buss drove up hurriedly, two trunks, four bandboxes, a valise, several shawls, finally the Dolliper herself got out, to the amazement of us all.

ADOBE FIRE-PLACE.

"I was afraid I'd be too late to catch you," she said, puffing and blowing. "How do you do, my dear (kissing June on both cheeks)? How you *have* improved. And *you* (meaning the Governor, and holding on to his hand). *You!* Why I wouldn't have believed it. You've been born again, haven't you? It's incredible. Then you're going to the Springs—there's no need of my stopping here at all. Here, you (to driver), put these things back. Good lands, what a time I had getting word to you! But there's no use worrying over that now. Our party's made up. Come along Governor, we'll get to the Springs to dinner, and they *have* dinners up there, I tell *you!*"

With this she took the Governor's arm. At least June says she *took* it; but I thought he *offered* her his arm. He pretended to be very glad to see her, and they went off together. June and I following after.

"Did you come to stay long?"

"Oh dear, yes, as long as you do," says the Dolliper, looking round kindly upon us. "I'm going to show you the country. Don't mind us if we talk business occasionally."

I felt June tremble with indignation; but she smiled and said she was delighted.

I don't believe it. There wasn't anybody delighted but the Governor.

UNDER THE WALLS.

With dreamful eyes my spirit lies
Under the walls of Paradise.
—Read.

If the reader will take the map of the United States and look at the tinted square lying directly west of the State of Kansas and marked Colorado, he will see the Rocky Mountain range dividing it north and south almost in the middle. The Territory is thus partitioned into three domains. First, the eastern upland slope, descending toward the Mississippi, and drained by the Arkansas River. Second, the intermediate mountainous district, and third, the western or Pacific slope. These three divisions of country are essentially unlike in climate, topography, scenery, and natural resources. The eastern slope lies forever in the sun, sheltered from the Pacific Ocean by the wall of porphyry and gneiss that rises ten thousand feet into the air, and from the still more disagreeable Atlantic by the dry plains that stretch away eastward for at least two hundred miles.

A general description of this exceptional tract would make it an upland plateau watered by streams of melting snow, and beautifully diversified as it approaches the mountains by mesa and valley, through which the cotton-wood and the lesser flora spring in abundance. It is the land of sunshine, of a perpetually dry air, and the one spot on the continent where the east wind does not harass the invalid.

ADOBE OVEN.

Here, under the walls of Paradise, one is perfectly safe from either ocean. The asthmatic feel the aerial influence at once. The debilitated are spurred by an invisible hand. There is no dew at night. The moon looks kindly down through a crystalline sky, and the sun shines with an Italian effulgence. From Pueblo, north, Colorado Springs is only forty-two miles off. We arrive there leisurely in three hours on the Narrow Gauge Railway, and then we are face to face with Pike's Peak, only a pleasant walk from the Garden of the Gods, and fairly in the center of the Sanitarium.

Here all the conditions of life are new and inspiriting. The town itself lies under the mountains on a sunny plain. The ice-cold streams from the snow-covered peaks bubble through its streets, and irrigate the fields. Here there is no winter as the dweller on the Atlantic coast has known it, and no summer as he has learned to dread it, but an equable, eternal spring. He shall fancy himself on the plains of Lombardy, or in the valley of the Lauterbrunnen, and the mornings will not chill him, nor the evenings chase him with unkindly breath within-doors. All the airy influences of Nature are beneficent and tender, and a new electrical stimulus spurs him into activity.

She has wrapped her grandeur in the most varied beauty of color, she pours her medicine at his feet from every valley, and drops it in like incense from every zephyr. Does this sound rhapsodical? Pray, remember that I have written it where one cannot breathe without taking in

ozone, and cannot drink without imbibing carbonic acid gas. Where the very fish, flesh and fowl are whipped gamy and fresh from the mountain trout-streams, or hunted in the fastnesses.

The pressure of such an atmosphere as weighs you down is gone at an elevation of six thousand three hundred and seventy feet. Shall not the emotions come to the surface with the blood?

Here, indeed, one can watch the varying moods and complexions of the mobile mountain and never grow tired of watching. Changing with every hour, he still looks calmly down out of the same grandeur. Morning hangs her auroral

THE MOUNTAIN BROOK.

softness on his crags; noonday deepens the thousand shadows of his furrowed face, and sunset flings a roseate glory over his snowy crown, but nothing robs him of the awful majesty and sovereignty of his character.

The town of Colorado Springs lies upon a natural level, close to the foot-hills and facing the range. Between it and the mountains extends the table-land called the Mesa, which is at once a meadow and a terrace, sweeping up to the rocky ascent with graceful curves, and cut here and there with the rivulets that brawl down from the heights. Standing upon the veranda of the hotel which faces the peaks, one cannot, even after a week's familiarity with the scene, entirely disabuse himself of the illusion, that the picturesque and serrated wall lifting itself far above him, is more than a stone's throw away. The inevitable and irresistible impulse of every new-comer is to walk over to the mountains before breakfast. The invariable result is, if he undertakes it, that he will not be back to dinner. It is five miles to the foot-hills, and ten at least to Pike's Peak proper. But with one leg of an imaginary pair of compasses stuck into the hotel, you may with the other describe a ten-mile circle, such as we sometimes see upon city maps, which will inclose most of the natural wonders of this range that have been celebrated the world over.

Pike's Peak, the Ute Pass, the Falls of the Fountain, the Garden of the Gods, Glen Eyrie, Monument Park, Cheyenne Canyon, Manitou and the Mineral Springs are all easily accessible, and are held by the people of this town to be their natural perquisites.

Manitou Glen, lying in the mouth of the Ute Pass, and already turned into a fashionable watering-place, is, to my mind, the most attractive, if not the most stupendous, of these resorts. Nothing so thoroughly Swiss in its wildness and rocky beauty have I anywhere seen. And it is, difficult, as you enter it, to avoid listening for the tinkle of the Alpine cattle-bell, and the echo of the *ranz des vaches*. But its pictorial interest is, when you come to penetrate it far enough broader, deeper, and more varied than anything Switzerland has to offer. The volcanic agency has massed the primitive colors of the earth so as to defy description; the red sandstone, the porphyry, the gleaming granite, against which the white limestone stands out in curious relief; the moss-grown bowlders, the splendid seams of red oxide and ochrous earth,—make an *ensemble* of pigments that is wonderfully fascinating. All these hues are softened and complemented by the varying tints of a luxurious vegetation. The Fountain Creek comes tunefully down the pass, through chasms and over precipices. Pinyon, pine, cedar, birch and hemlock shade the road in overhanging groves, and mark the timber lines upon the heights a thousand feet above us in successive belts of color. The wild clematis and the Virginia creeper festoon the natural arcades with their tracery, and myriads of aromatic shrubs and wild flowers make the underbrush and the sod brilliant with their dyes, and load the air with their perfumes.

The moment we leave the mesa and enter this valley, we are upon enchanted ground. In one instant we have passed from the shadowless and voiceless void to the sacred penetralia, where every natural agency is leagued in the witchery of beauty. South of us rises, eight thousand

SODA SPRINGS AND CLIFF HOUSE, MANITOU.

feet above, the snow-filled ravines and glittering pinnacles of Pike's Peak. East of us, a mere glimpse of the yellow and level meads of the great plain. All about us, that indescribable charm of wildness not yet tamed into conventional lines.

It is here that we meet upon the rocky road-side, just as we have experienced the first thrill of delight common to all men in complete isolation, with the luxuriant hotel and Spring House, nestling with a true watering-place elegance of piazza and drives, right in the lap of solitude.

It is here, too, that we encounter the mineral springs. They are six in number, and vary in temperature from 43° to 56° F., and are strongly charged with carbonic acid. They are respectively called "The Shoshone," "The Navajoe," "The Manitou," "The Ute Soda," "The Iron Ute," and "The Little Chief." The waters have, from time immemorial, enjoyed a curative reputation among the Indians, and many are the romantic legends that have been left behind as to their origin and purpose.

Professor Loew, of the Wheeler Expedition, has published an analysis which shows that they resemble the springs of Ems, and excel those of Spa. I cannot help thinking, in spite of all the testimony, that the great medicinal virtue of this place is in its air. A balsamic breath blows forever down the Pass from the pines, and one has only to watch the invalids climbing the rocks, driving over the plains, and making long excursions into the ever new mysteries of the range, to perceive that they are spurred and animated by vital influences that are rare.

A pretty wide experience of watering-places enables me to speak with conviction, when I say that I believe this spot will, in time, become a national resort. It can be reached now in four days from New-York, by the Atchison, Topeka & Santa Fé Road. Its position, its surroundings and its climatic conditions surpass those of any place in this country. Within half an hour's walk is "The Garden of the Gods." Lying behind it is the main range of the Rocky Mountains, which furnishes ever new surprises to the adventurous explorer, and offers all kinds of game to the sportsman. Excellent brook-trout, ptarmigan, or Rocky Mountain quail, red-tail deer, and duck, snipe and grouse, to say nothing of antelope and an occasional cinnamon bear, are the standard temptations. I ought to say here that,

GRACE GREENWOOD'S COTTAGE, MANITOU.

unlike Switzerland, the mountains are in this vicinity entirely accessible. Our party, in which there were four ladies, penetrated the Ute Pass a distance of over two miles, and ascended to an elevation of nine thousand feet without any difficulty. We afterward found an easy path up the Cheyenne Canyon, and an excellent carriage-road to the top of the Grand Canyon. The forests of pine timber do not cease until an elevation of eleven thousand five hundred feet is reached; whereas, in Switzerland, they disappear at six thousand feet. I am told that at Mount Lincoln mining is carried on all winter at an altitude of over fourteen thousand feet, which is as high as the "Jungfrau."

To the tourist "The Garden of the Gods" will probably ever remain the most prominent attraction of this place. Before I set out for that celebrated natural museum, I rapped at the door of a quaint little cottage, perched up like a wren's nest, over the brook in the pass. One cannot look at its exterior and resist the temptation to make a call. Unfortunately for me, Grace Greenwood was not at home. However, after inspecting as much of the nest as was accessible, I felt my respect for the lady's independence materially heightened. If she had possessed less she would have built an ornamental château at Long Branch, and then lived in New-York to escape from it. She was probably, at the time I called, making a visit to the United States Signal Station in the clouds near by, or had gone to Denver on her mule to do her shopping.

GOD'S GARDEN.

Bottomless vales and boundless floods,
And chasms and caves and Titan woods
With forms that no man can discover.
—Poe.

It was not enough that we should visit the Garden of the Gods by daylight; June insisted that it should be done by moonlight.

It is one of those natural parks where Thor and Boreas seem to have done all the hammering and chiseling, after a greater than either had shut the domain in with an upturned stratum. The gate, as you approach the entrance, is by far the finest part of the exhibition.

If you will imagine a bed of red and gray sandstone, gypsum and limestone, from twenty to fifty feet thick, five hundred feet broad and half a mile long, turned on edge and broken in the middle so as to leave a gap of a hundred feet wide, you will get a general idea of the ridge which forms this wall and gate-way. But you cannot possibly have any conception of the intricate modeling, the grotesque forms into which the elements have worn the surface, nor of the splendid hues, partly integral and partly laid on by the artist hand of time. To the cultivated eye, the form is lost in the blaze of pigments. When the painter first sees it he pauses in astonishment at what appears to be a stupendous and idealess poem of color. From a little distance the façade, where it does not rise scarlet and maroon against the greens of the hills behind, runs into a veined and patched mosaic of chalcedony and onyx.

As the beholder draws closer he sees that it is the graining and enameling of the elements on a superb ground, and then he perceives also, that a thousand demons with preternatural chisels were probably doomed to work at these fantastic pinnacles and niches and pedestals for ages— left, indeed, to their own grotesque fancies to shape and scoop and polish the eternal bastions into the strangest devices—only they could not cease from their work. Nothing short of the fancy of a Coleridge can write the demoniac history of the gates. But I can readily see that any man, even without aboriginal blood in him, would drop into a poetical fetishism if he lived here long and had few companions, other than the whirling eagles which build their nests along the parapet, and rear the young symbols of the Republic in the upper frieze.

But to see it at night is another thing. Then if the moon be full, the demon of the mountain writhes in the mysterious light, the phantom moves on his pedestal and shakes his shroud at you. Your horses grow restive, and all those strange monuments seem, indeed, to be imprisoned ghosts.

June well said that Poe must have visited this place in one of his disembodied moments. And then, to heighten the effect, she declaimed one of his cheerful verses:

" By a route obscure and lonely
Haunted by ill angels only,
    Where an Eidolon named Night
    On a black throne reigns upright,
I have reached these lands but newly
From an ultimate dim Thule—
    From a wild, weird clime—
    Out of Space, out of Time."

"Don't you remember," she said, in a whisper, "that he acknowledges in ' Ulalume,'

" ' Here, once through an alley Titanic
    Of cypress, I roamed with my soul
    Of cypress, with Psyche my soul,
    Those were days when my heart was
        volcanic
        As the scoriæ rivers that roll ?' "

The fact is, Colorado is a land of wonders. A week at the springs hardly suffices to see them all.

June's note-book contains, along with a number of excellent pencil-sketches, the following memoranda, which are better summaries than I can make:

U. S. SIGNAL STATION, SUMMIT OF PIKE'S PEAK.

"Visitors must not fail to visit Monument Park. It is only ten miles north of the springs, and contains some wonderful monoliths that are curiously cut by the wind.

"The Petrified Forest is too far away for a hurried visit, and one has to cross the foot-hills to get at it. However, they get fine moss-agates who go there.

"Glen Eyrie, the residence of General Palmer, is at the mouth of Queens Canyon. The Canyon is worth a visit.

"There is a good bridle-path part of the way up Pike's Peak. Regular ascents are made by parties from the Manitou House. The U. S. Signal Station is at the summit, and the view, when the clouds do not interfere, is sublime.

"There is a half-way house on the ascent, where the tourist gets excellent refreshment, and can rest. Those who have climbed Mont Blanc will find the journey up Pike's Peak mere child's play, though it is 14,000 feet high.

"The roads in Colorado are natural boulevards, and the finest horses in the world can be obtained at moderate prices. I attribute the health of the visitors at the springs, in great measure, to this fact: They ride and walk incessantly—thus living in the open air.

"I wish I had Poe's talent for half an hour. I'd write a description of a star-lit night here. I shall remember its 'crystalline delight' as long as I live. The only disagreeable feature is the leaving it and going indoors to bed.   The society at the springs is excellent, cultivated people from all parts of the world make up the visitors, and they so far adopt themselves to the Western customs as to leave many of their conventional notions, and their exclusiveness, at home.   The air, the freedom and the sight-seeing make it a continual holiday.

"Don't fail to take a run up to Denver City by the Denver and Rio Grande Narrow Gauge Railroad, which skirts the base of the mountains, runs through chasms and gulches, and along ledges, every one of which furnishes a new sensation.

"Denver is the smartest city west of the Mississippi, and once there, the tourist who has come through the garden of Kansas can go on to California, if he chooses, by the Union Pacific.   In fact, I believe, very many California passengers, in order to avoid the long and dreary ride from Omaha to Cheyenne, now come by the way of Pueblo.*

"Tourists with a geologic taste will find Colorado Springs rich in specimens. Agate, chalcedony, onyx, topaz, rock crystal, jasper, fossils, spar, gold, silver, galena, malachite and carnelian can be picked up, or bought at the museums for a trifle.   I saw an agate at the office of Col. McAllister, that weighed five hundred pounds.   It was, I believe, to be cut and sent to the Centennial.   Up in the gulches

ROCKS IN MONUMENT PARK.

near Denver, they occasionally find rubies and garnets, but they are rare.

"I lay last night, for an hour, listening to the bubbling of the ice-water under my window.   It was the stream from the melted snows on the mountains.   These cold rivulets are led through all the streets.   It reminded me of Morris's verse:

> " ' Water shouts a glad hosanna,
>   Bubbles up the Earth to bless!
>   Cheers us like a precious manna,
>   In the Western wilderness.' "

* Parties going to California can visit all the famous resorts of Colorado, *en route*, by asking for tickets from New-York to San Francisco via the Atchison, Topeka & Santa Fé Railroad, passing through the Kansas Valley, touching Pueblo, Colorado Springs, Denver and Cheyenne, and thence via the Union Pacific Railroad.   Through tickets to the Pacific Coast by this route can only be obtained of Cook, Son & Jenkins, 261 Broadway, or at any of their offices in Europe or America.

THE GRAND CANYON.

We, too, have tracked by star-proof trees,
The tempest of the Thyiades,
Scare the loud night on hills that hid,
Outchide the north wind if it chid,
And hush the torrent-tongued ravines
With thunders of their tambourines.
—SWINBURNE.

"EVERY THING has been conquered but the Grand Canyon," I said.

June was thoughtful. "How high do you say Pike's Peak is?" she asked.

"14,336 feet," I answered.

"And people sometimes risk their lives in going up?"

"Yes, I suppose so; people who have heart-troubles risk a great deal in the rarified atmosphere."

"Well," said June, "we must get the Dolliper up there. Do you think her heart's affected?"

I looked at her with amazement; she kept on, thoughtfully:

"Fourteen thousand feet above the level of the sea. I wish it was fourteen thousand feet beneath!"

"My dear girl!" I exclaimed, "why this unusual fiendishness?"

"Listen a moment," said the dear girl, sitting down by the side of a soda spring in the glen where we had wandered. "That woman has been talking to the Governor about his Kansas land; she has coaxed him into the belief that they can together make some kind of a magnificent enterprise by a partnership in hemp. He rather likes the idea, and as the Dolliper flatters him, he lets her have her own way. Don't you see that we must push that woman down a canyon, or else——"

"Well," I cried, "else?"——

"Or else you must help me to outwit her."

"How?"

"By insisting that the land belongs to me. I've won it. If you and Bellamy stand by me, we can beat her."

"What will you do with the land?" I asked; "sell it?"

"No; cultivate it."

"Then I'm yours. There comes the Dolliper now."

"She's looking for a fresh mineral spring," said June. "It's her weakness; she smells of every puddle, to see if it's not soda water, and I've been trying to persuade her that there is a perennial spring of ginger beer on the top of Pike's Peak. But if you stand by me, she shall live, for she shall be made miserable."

That very day we left the Springs to pay a visit to the Grand Canyon of the Arkansas. Every one of the party regretted leaving the delightful vicinity of Manitou. But the tourist's fate hurried us on.

We proceeded to Canyon City (which is a little town eighty miles south of the Springs) by the Denver and Rio Grande road, and there we took a conveyance to the top of the canyon, twelve

miles west of the town, and there Ben joined us again. After a toilsome drive in the mountains of three hours, we turned into a grove of pine and pinyon, a gnarled, knobby Arcadia. "Hold on!" shouted the driver, as some of the party, with the usual alertness of excursionists, sprang out of the vehicle and began roaming about. "Wait, danger!" He tied his horses carefully, and took his crowbar out of the carriage. "This 'ere's the canyon," said he. "Mind your eye!" We could see through the trees a number of rocks lying as if in a field. Guided by the driver, we approached them. And then it became suddenly apparent to all of us that these rocks were the brim of a chasm two thousand feet deep, and nearly a mile wide. Those of us who approached the edge and looked down, drew back with bated breath. Two thousand feet straight down is a view not often accorded to man, and it takes some time to adjust the strongest nerves to the con-

GARDEN OF THE GODS.

ditions. The brink of this awful gulf is ragged and broken. Great crumbling projections of rock offer precarious points of sight, and little ledges that look as solid as the earth behind you, disclose to your eye when you crawl to the edge, the thrilling fact that you are out upon what appears to be the rotten half of a broken arch. One seemingly secure promontory ended in a level platform of granite, far out beyond the jagged line, and upon this rim one of the ladies was discovered standing with her toes over the edge, and her dress fluttering in the mountain breeze. Just as the party called to her to come down, the driver caught her suddenly by the arm and pulled her back. Scarcely had she stepped from the granite out-look, when the man put the point of his crowbar into a crack of the huge stone and dislodged the whole mass with comparatively little effort, sending it down the abyss with the roar and smoke of an exploded cannon. Lying upon our stomachs, the whole party, with our chins projecting over the brink, looked far down into the curiously vertical perspective, and trembled. There at the bottom roared and foamed the Arkansas River, dwindled now to a thread of wrinkled silver, the trees upon its shores looking like weeds. While in this position our guide busied himself with his lever. With prodigious labor, he worked the enormous bowlders loose, and we saw them hurled downward, now exploding into fire and dust as they struck some projecting ledge, now roaring and hurtling with incalculable momentum through the timber, opening a swathe in the trees, filling the gorge with sharp echoes, and disappearing in the deep distance in clouds of atoms.

Strange sport this, but there is an undeniable fascination about it. This driver and guide is proof enough that the parties coming here expect this part of the entertainment, and I am told that they make up picnics in Canyon City and visit this spot with little other purpose than to dislodge the rocks. Delicate women, robust men and timid children will then stand in a group and listen with intense satisfaction and considerable awe at the devastation they make. I confess that the sport, aside from the pure exhibition of natural dynamics, seemed to me somewhat profane.

Some months ago the Atchison, Topeka & Santa Fé Railroad had one hundred men employed in the valley below cutting railroad ties and floating them down the Arkansas, and it was found necessary to post a polite notice among these trees, requesting tourists not to throw stones or play with avalanches. I asked the guide whether the visitors generally insisted on this Cyclopean sport, and he said the women almost always got it up and then made the most fuss about it. I wonder if the wanton exhibition of power is not characteristic of the sex. So far, no accidents that I could hear of have happened here.

Afterward, when seated under the trees enjoying our lunch, the roar of the wind through the canyon amazed us. Such unearthly diapason was surely never heard anywhere else. It was indeed the voice of the Almighty, and I feel how puny must be any human attempt to characterize those tones with mere words. We exhaust our dynamic terms when we make reference to thunder, but here was an awful melody emitted from the larynx of mother earth—a stupendous monochord made by vibrating mountains. If ever you desire to hear an Æolian lute which breathes the solemn oratorio of creation in such tremulous passion-tones as make the soul shudder, or mount to a *Te Deum* on the airy gamut of atmospheres, come and sit passive a few moments by the side of this organ, which makes a cathedral of immensity.

"Tell us, somebody," cried June, brushing a Rocky Mountain grasshopper from her sandwich, "how this chasm was made."

"Ah," says Bellamy, with mug in one hand and a slice of ham in the other, "you'll have to apostrophize the elements."

> "No forest fell,
> When thou didst build, no quarry sent its stones
> To enrich thy walls, but thou didst hew the floods,
> And make thy marble of the glassy wave."

"Good poetry, but bad geology," says Ben. "Water had very little to do with it. Agassiz says it was rent at one upheaval, and buried afterward in six thousand feet of ice for a million years."

"Then," says June, with a woman's charming impatience, "don't let us go into its history."

The Governor (with a sardine by the tail). No, we have other business of more importance. We've reached the end of our tether, and now you young folks ought to be thinking of going home.

Ben. Young folks! We scorn the idea of going home without you.

Mrs. Dolliper (pallidly munching a Canyon City biscuit). I have induced him to stay in Kansas and go into business again.

The Governor (using the supplement of a New-York *Herald* for a napkin). Yes, I think some of trying to utilize that Kansas land. The climate has not only restored my health, but my sense of duty and my ambition.

June. You never lost your sense of duty. You gave the land away by promise, and I claim it now. It will take something more than Kansas influence, or St. Louis influence either, to make you break your word!

[Tumultuous applause from Ben, Bellamy and me, which volleyed through the canyon and startled the Governor with the idea that nature sympathized with us.]

The Dolliper saw the peril, and tried to get an adjournment. But majorities have no more hearts than corporations.

"Bless my soul!" said the Governor, reprovingly. "I said the one who got the most information. That's a point that it will take several years to decide."

"Can be done in two minutes," responded June. "I've got my vouchers in my book here. Take a vote."

"Aye, aye," shouted all her confederates, "a vote, a vote!"

Ben then made a little speech. He said: "May it please your Excellency, the only contingency that could in any case destroy June's claim to this estate grew out of the rivalry of other competitors. I have the honor to inform you, that, fully satisfied of the futility of further competition, we have all withdrawn in her favor,

OLD FOGY STAGE-DRIVER.

and trust that you will soon be convinced, as we are, that she is entitled to the property. I believe she can justify her claim at this moment."

"Try me," cried June; "I've got two hundred pages of information in my book. I can read it in less than three hours and a half."

"My dear," said the Dolliper, "you'll exhaust yourself. Don't."

"Read, read!" cried Ben and all the rest of us.

"No, no!" broke in the Governor. "Print it, print it. We'll read it in a book."

"But how am I to prove my claim?" asked the intrepid girl.

"Here, we'll have a competitive examination," replied the Governor. "Mr. Bellamy and Mrs. Dolliper shall be umpires. What are the chief products of Kansas?"

"Corn, cattle, cow-boys, and contentment," said Ben.

"Railroads," said Bellamy, looking as ignorant as possible.

"School-houses," said I.

"Kansas," said June, pluming herself, "produces astonishment. She does it by means of her winter wheat, of which she grew in 1875, 10,046,116 bushels, that brought at the depot, $9,457,559.17. She has altogether, 4,749,900.89 acres under cultivation and pasture, which in that year produced products to the value of $43,970,494.28, exclusive of live stock. If you like that sort of thing, I can give you plenty of it."

BALANCE-ROCK.

"I confess it's rather tedious to me," said the Dolliper.

"Oh, we just revel in it," added Ben and the other conspirators.

"Proceed," said June, calmly. "Try me on the meteorology, ornithology, geognosy, oryktog-nosy. I am a fountain of information: tap me with a question, and I'll spout statistics by the hour."

I think the Governor saw by this time that he was out-maneuvered. He made one or two feeble attempts to ask questions, but they were met promptly with such a volume of facts, that he was not rash enough to go on. It was more convenient to acknowledge that June had won, than to let her prove it. Still he could not resist the temptation to try her with one or two other conundrums.

CATTLE-DROVE IN THE MOUNTAINS.

GOLD.

"'Over the mountains
Of the moon,
Down the valley of the shadow
Ride, boldly ride,'
The shade replied,
If you seek for Eldorado.'"

A SHREWD twinkle came into the Governor's eye, as he asked: "How about the gold fields south of us? Come, that's what I want to know about."

"It was the gold fields of Southern Colorado, and the immense territory of Mexico, holding the oldest civilization on our continent, that shaped the A. T. & S. F. route," said June. "Why, commerce, whether on the ocean or on the prairie, has its own channels. There was a road laid out by Col. Sibley, in 1822, from Missouri to Santa Fé. It was called the Santa Fé trail. It was one of the richest highways on the continent. Ben and I came across it when we were galloping over Kansas,—an old weed-grown road-bed, fifty feet wide,—and we followed it for ten miles, just to see the old fords, and imagine the ambuscades where the teamsters fought for their lives, and the women were dragged out of the wagons at night by savages. It was an early necessity of commerce, and the iron trail that has taken its place, with palace cars, heads for the same objective point, and for hundreds of miles follows the same route.

"This is the gold region. Directly south is the Decatur District on the south fork of the Alamosa. Not more than five miles west is the head of the San Juan River, and within a radius of fifty miles we have what are, without doubt, the richest mineral lands in the United States. Geologists tell me that there is no longer any doubt that the whole of the Sangre de Cristo and Saguache ranges, are filled with gold-bearing quartz, silver, galena and coal. One thing appears to be beyond all dispute, and that is, wherever in this region capital has employed skilled labor, and the proper appliances to work the raw material, gold has been turned out in paying quantities. One does not here encounter the lawless hordes which, in the infancy of gold mining, made California so notorious. The era of nuggets and gulch-washing has passed. The solitary adventurer finds little encouragement here other than the chance of locating a claim, and selling it afterward. As for working it advantageously single-handed, that is an impossibility. These rich seams are enormous fissures, almost vertical in their dip, and filled with half a hundred different ores, of which the precious metals seldom form more than one-fourth per cent. To work them requires metallurgical skill. To find the gold is one thing, to extract it is another. The miner was once a finder. The whole successful force of this country is engaged in extracting.

"I believe it is a law that obtains everywhere, that Nature only yields her riches, whether they be mineralogical or vegetable, in return for labor expended. There is reason to believe, on purely a priori grounds, that she will yield more in this country than in any other. It has taken about twenty-five years of teaching to get this lesson well into our heads. The first crusaders who rushed across the continent to California and Pike's Peak, believed in luck. They expected to pick up the gold before somebody else found it. The popular idea was that Nature had smelted and assayed and run it into bricks, which she had poked away among her rocks for the longest-winded and most desperate chaps to stumble over. You can follow their trails now by the graves and the bones across Kansas and Colorado. They rushed into the wilderness and helped to make it green with their carcasses. Then came the era of speculation, of mismanagement, dishonesty and pecuniary crimes. Mines were bought at a thousand times their value, and stocked at ten times the purchase. Incompetent but audacious men were sent out to take charge. The wrong kind of mills were transported at enormous expense, and they stand to-day all over the country wrecks of iron, to attest the stupendous stupidity of the people who had the fever, and little else. Over six hundred million dollars, I am told, has been subscribed to milling and mining schemes since the discovery of gold in California.

"About 60 per cent. of this sum was paid in cash—the balance remains on paper.

"Prospecting for claims in this country still is the most exciting and romantic feature of the gold-hunting business. A certain class of men, fitted only for an adventurous and nomadic life, make this a business, and there are many strange stories told, just as they have been told before, of the same class in California, of men discovering rich deposits, staking out their claims and then bartering the whole thing for a horse or a pistol in a debauch attending their good luck, or what is still more common, losing the claim at a game of cards, and the next day setting out to discover another.

"What Colorado needs above all else is manufactures. Her mineral resources are inexhaustible. Every thing of solid value that the bowels of the earth produce comes to the surface here, or can be dug out with the smallest amount of energy. But she needs organized labor, productive capital, resident capitalists. Since the Atchison, Topeka & Santa Fé road has been completed to Pueblo, a great change has taken place. Milling stock and agricultural implements have penetrated almost to the Mexican frontier. Engineers and millwrights are examining the Rio Grande and the thousand other streams, and before another census is taken the whole of this country will have taken on a new aspect.

"There are 4,500 silver mines in San Juan.

"As you go westward from Pueblo through the Wet Mountain Valley, you reach Mosco Pass in the Sangre de Cristo Mountains, and about seventy-five miles from the present terminus of the Atchison, Topeka & Santa Fé Railroad. Here are the celebrated Sangre de Cristo gold quartz mines, extending in a belt from near Mosco Pass forty miles north. Gold was first discovered on this range in November, 1874, since which time large quantities of gold quartz have been taken out, running from $50 to $500 per ton, while one lead has, within the last three months, taken out gold quartz assaying upward of $40,000 per ton.

"In the San Juan country there are thousands of mines located, and to be located, which carry a higher grade ore than the Monte Cristo, which might be worked with still greater profit, if facilities for treatment and transportation were ample. The ores, as worked in San Juan last season, run from $150 to $2,000 per ton. The highest average of ores in one run of Green & Co's smelter at Silverton, San Juan county, was $849.44, while the average run for the entire season was $220 per ton. No silver mining country in the world can make such a showing. The usual cost of taking out ores in San Juan is from $8 to $10 per ton. The profits may be less than given above on low grade ores for the present, but at no distant day the thousands and thousands of veins that for over a hundred miles interlace and weave together with cords of silver the main mountain ranges in San Juan, will attract capital and labor, and the development of this vast treasure-house will, ere long, be known as one of the chief industries of the United States. Is there any thing else you would like to know ?"

WOLVERINE.

"Yes," said the Governor, "I'd like to know where you got all this information."

Cries of "oh, oh," and "shame," from the majority, who never meant to divulge the fact that she got it from Ben.

"There's one other thing I'd like to say," remarked June. "It's this—we can readily verify my statements by taking one of Barlow & Sanderson's new coaches and going down there."*

This was a clever stroke. The Governor had a mortal dread of a stage-coach (I believe he had been overturned, in his youth, on the Alleghanies), and as Ben and Bellamy immediately seconded the suggestion, he had to acknowledge that the statement did not need verifying.

* The only direct railroad route into the San Juan country is by the Atchison, Topeka & Santa Fé Railroad. By taking this route the distance is shorter than any other line by 143 miles. Connections with this road are made from all points east at Kansas City or Atchison.

This great line of road commences at both of the above-named points on the Missouri river and extends 684 miles, via Topeka, the capital of Kansas, thence south-west to the Arkansas river, and thence up the fertile and beautiful valley of the Arkansas to Pueblo.

HOME AGAIN.

"Behind they saw the snow-cloud tossed
By many an icy horn:
Before, warm valleys wood embossed
And green with vines and corn."

PIKE'S PEAK was behind us, we were homeward bound.

"I'm going to make a book of it all," said June to me in the cars, when the other members of our party had gone off to smoke.

She had accumulated material enough certainly, but who would buy it when made into a book?

"Buy it?" exclaimed the enthusiastic girl—"I'll give it away; circulate it through the benevolent societies of England, Ireland, and Scotland, and thus do something for my race. I don't want to make money with a book. I can make enough off my farm. I want to show my fellow-man how he can go and do likewise.

"So long as land is given away, the needy ought to know it; especially as it is better land than that which commands the highest price. So long as men suffer and die with disease, they ought to hear of a land where they can live and grow strong."

"Excuse me," said I, "but aren't you a little extravagant in your statements?"

"No, sir" (with decision, and producing her note-book). "They give land away to industrious people in Kansas if they are too poor to buy it. Let me read you the substance of the Timber-Tree Law of Kansas: 'Any person who is twenty-one years of age, or the head of a family, and a citizen of the United States, can get title to forty, eighty, or one hundred and sixty acres of land by planting one-fourth of the land in timber-trees not more than twelve feet apart each way. If they take one hundred and sixty acres, they will be required to plant forty acres, and they must break ten acres the first year, ten acres the second year, and twenty acres the third year; and plant ten acres the second year, ten the third and twenty acres the fourth year. They must make oath that the land is wanted for the cultivation of timber as aforesaid. They must make proof within eleven years that they have cultivated the timber at least eight years. The fees will be about $12.00 to $15.00. Many claims can be purchased in this county that can be paid for by planting timber in this way.' Now as for salubriousness, I made a special study of it in Colorado, and I interviewed all the scientific men I met. The conclusion is this: Colorado, for weak lungs, bronchitis, rheumatism, gout and those diseases that have their origin in malaria, is a certain cure. It is the only place in the world where a man can get along comfortably with one lung so long as he has got two legs. All forms of phthisis are benefited by the air. This is not a random statement; I make it from actual experience. The dry, electric air of such places as Manitou, to say nothing of the effects of the waters, has made it the resort of invalids who have tried Italy, Minnesota, Florida and Havana. It is far superior in its relief to chronic bronchial and rheumatic troubles to California, because here one escapes the cold, wet night-winds from the ocean, and because Manitou lies in a valley amidst the mountains, at an elevation of six thousand three hundred and seventy feet, and is unlike the resorts of Switzerland in its accessibility and its close communication with a country covered with growing crops and flourishing towns. The altitude of the country is something that the people east appear to have very vague notions about.

"They forget that Colorado is in the clouds—a kind of heaven above their comprehension. Let me read you this table of heights:

Denver City........................ 5,317	feet above the sea.
Colorado Springs.......................5,720	" "
Pueblo Springs........................4,400	" "
Canyon City Springs...................4,700	" "
Manitou...............................6,370	" "

"This is a nice sliding scale for people who wish to adjust their lungs to a particular rarification. And then if they desire to go higher—as men always do—we have adjacent and accessible:

Pike's Peak 14,336	feet above the sea.
Mount Harvard...... .... .14,270	" "
Mount Lincoln 14,145	" "

"The parks in these mountain ranges are elysiums sheltered from storms, open to the sun, fed with mountain streams and alive with game."

"What kind of game?" I asked, anxious to see if this encyclopedic girl had gone into zoölogy also.

A MOUNTAIN COYOTE.

"What kinds! Buffalo, the best and biggest game that runs, is plentiful on the plains, I saw no less than three hunting parties made up at Pueblo. Antelope, coyote, or prairie wolves, occasionally the gray or timber wolf, red fox, elk, red-tailed deer, mountain goat, cinnamon bears and even grizzlies. As for grouse and water-fowl, they're too thick to bother with, as you can see."

"But after all," said I, "Colorado is a country for invalids. I cannot see how it is going to feed itself. It is true, Pueblo and other towns have made irrigation successful on a limited scale, by availing themselves of the streams from the mountains, but that plan, picturesque as it is, will not do for wheat-fields; besides, the country will be equally divided between invalids and miners, who are the most voracious eaters in the world."

"Well," replied June, "I said something like that to a Colorado man. I took down his reply; here it is: ' You air perfckly correk. We ain't hankerin' after agriculter. It wouldn't do us much good ef we was, with that air paster layin' out there (sweeping his brown hand broadly, so as to indicate the whole of Kansas). Hev you bin over that patch ?'

"I said, ' Yes.'

" ' Then you've been in the gardin of men. We ain't got nuthin but gardins of gods fur to show. But I calkerlate, when we git the gold out o' natur's bowels, there won't much milk and honey run to waste for the want of a market. No, marm; it'll climb this way. Why, you kin talk about your gardins—that air State's a regular *cornicupio*, with the big end turned this way. In ten year, you'll find the human race coming to Colorady to live, and expectin' Kansas to help 'em through. It'll do it! It'll do it! All we can promise 'em is to fill their pockets and their lungs. The folks down there'll fill their bellies, you bet, and have somethin' over.'

"This homely speech was not devoid of sagacity. The prosperity of the two States is, in a certain sense, guaranteed by their absolute difference. One produces and the other will consume.

"The amazing richness of this whole mountain range, not alone in gold and silver, but in all the other metals, and in coal,—a richness that grows upon the sense as one passes south,—convinces me that a measureless commerce is yet to spring up with the South-

ROCKY MOUNTAIN QUAIL—WINTER AND SUMMER PLUMAGE.

west, and that the country about Santa Fé, once the objective point of those numberless traders who risked their lives upon the plains, will sooner or later be one of the busiest domains within the borders of the Union.

" The whole of the tract known as San Juan is literally alive with the pioneer adventurers who seek a newly opened mining country. Every one is digging, and every one, by digging, can make money. But what the country needs is an open road to the capitalist, the machinist and the trader. It is in want of mills and markets; these the railroad alone will supply. To reach San Juan now, the traveler and the miner must ride for a hundred miles, at least, in a stage-coach, or upon a mule. With such primitive means of access, it is not strange that the tourist seldom ventures with his pencil beyond Canyon City. But even at that point, he observes that the Atchison, Topeka & Santa Fé road, already surveyed to the Rio Grande, will, in a very short time, connect Mexico with Missouri, closely and commercially, as the early Santa Fé traders sought, and in their primitive way, did indeed connect them.

"Nature, no less than traffic, appears to have indicated this route. The other lines which run further north, look primarily to California. The Santa Fé road aims at Colorado and the Southwest, a domain which, more than any other, is at this moment engaging the attention of the capitalist, as well as the wonder-hunter and adventurer. I found throughout Colorado a genuine interest in this railroad which is to be the great channel of nourishment and of emigration. Perhaps I should say that a ride in a buggy of a hundred miles, over the farming country in Kansas, led me to believe that the producers of that State are fully aware of their relations to the road, whose policy has been from the outset to encourage every kind of industry by fair rates, and by offering every reasonable inducement both to settlers and to residents.*

"If the remaining projected route to the South is completed as thoroughly and as durably as the line now reaching Pueblo, the West, I believe, will have reason to feel proud of one highway conscientiously constructed in the interest of the community."

After this copious extract from her book, June closed her album, the authoress vanished, and the colloquial woman was once more herself.

"O dear," she said, "there is Mrs. Dolliper, all alone; I'm afraid I've neglected her. Ever since that Canyon picnic, she's worn a crushed aspect. I suppose you know she is going on to New-York with us?"

"No!"

"Yes; Centennial, ostensibly. To stay with us and talk hemp, really."

"After we get her there, we'll coax her to destroy herself by going to Long Branch."

"O dear, no;" answered June, "I'll get her to lend me ten thousand dollars, and we'll come out and cultivate that farm. I think she'll do it."

"Then you do not want to push her down a canyon?"

"No; if she'll help me get my book out, we'll carry her down in a palanquin."

I do not know what June will say when she reads this book. It's so inferior to hers—lacks the fine fancy, the poetic gush, and as she would say, the thoughts that burn, and words that—what d'ye call it?

But she must give me credit, I am sure, for stealing all my facts and figures from her.

Since these pages were written, the Dolliper has been to the Centennial, and June has been made the mistress of two whole sections of Western land. In fact, the whole family is healthy, and wealthy, and wise. And it owes its present extraordinary felicity to its trip to Colorado.

---

* For the benefit of such readers as may desire further information regarding this wonderful country, the following list of officials and agents of the A. T. & S. F. R. R., is inserted, any one of whom will promptly respond to all inquiries by letter or in person regarding the country, the road, or its lands, and the cost of reaching this country from any part of the world. Thos. Nickerson, President; F. H. Peabody, Vice-President; Geo. L. Goodwin, Asst. Treasurer, all at Boston, Mass. C. F. Morse, General Supt.; E. Wilder, Sec'y & Treasurer; T. J. Anderson, General Passenger Agent; W. F. White, General Ticket Agent; M. L. Sargent, General Freight Agent; A. S. Johnson, Land Commissioner; Arthur Gorham, Ass't. Land Commissioner; C. B. Schmidt, General Foreign Agent, all of Topeka, Kansas. L. H. Nutting, General Eastern Agent, 239 Broadway, opposite Post Office, New-York; M. Solomon, N. W. Agent, 57 Dearborn St., Chicago, Ill.; S. B. Hynes, General Agent, and Eli Lewis, General Traveling Agent, 102 N. 4th St, St. Louis, Mo.; N. R. Warwick, General Southern Agent, 138 Vine St., Cincinnati, Ohio. Address or call on the agent nearest you.

www.ingramcontent.com/pod-product-compliance
Lightning Source LLC
Chambersburg PA
CBHW021246260626
47172CB00002B/852